P9-DDN-654

A unique blend of artistry, emotion, and natural history, this reassuring book is a must for horse lovers and is perfect for storytime sharing.

"Honda's full-spread watercolors, in wintry hues of ice blue and white, offer a sweeping, impressionistic panorama of the herd plowing through the drifts."
—*Publishers Weekly*

"The soft paintings combine with the simple text to bring a vanishing breed vividly to life. *Wild Horse Winter* is a wonderful book for reading aloud or for sharing, the story subtly parallels the growth of all creatures and underscores the strong bonds that exist between parent and child."
—*The Children's Bookwatch*

"Honda's dramatic paintings portray a stark existence and a harshness of weather and environment. . . . Some might consider this story an allegory for life, as the horses pursue a quest and reach their goal."
—*School Library Journal*

First published in the United States in 1992 by Chronicle Books. Copyright ©1991 by Tetsuya Honda. North American text based on the English translation by Susan Matsui—copyright ©1992 by Chronicle Books. All rights reserved. First published in Japan by Fukutake Publishing Company, Tokyo under the title "Dosanko-Uma No Fuyu."

Printed in Singapore.

Library of Congress Cataloging-in-Publication Data

Honda, Tetsuya.
    [Dosanko uma no fuyu.   English]
    Wild horse winter / Tetsuya Honda.
            p.   cm.
    Translation of: Dosanko uma no fuyu.
    Summary: A wild colt and his mother struggle to find food during a harsh winter.
    ISBN: 0-8118-0251-5 (hc)   ISBN: 0-8118-1211-1 (pb)
    1. Wild horses—Juvenile literature. 2. Foals—Juvenile literature. 3. Winter—Juvenile literature. [1. Wild horses. 2. Horses. 3. Winter.] I. Title.
SF360.H66   1992
599.72'5—dc20   92-14044
CIP

AC

Distributed in Canada by Raincoast Books
8680 Cambie Street, Vancouver, B.C. V6P 6M9

10 9 8 7 6 5 4

Chronicle Books
85 Second Street
San Francisco, California 94105

www.chroniclebooks.com

WILD HORSE WINTER

Tetsuya Honda

chronicle books · san francisco

One spring, a wild colt was born. All through the summer, he nibbled tender grasses. As the trees lost their leaves, he grew taller.

By the time the mountain peaks were dusted with snow, the colt had grown a thick coat to keep him warm during the cold months yet to come.

The days grew shorter. Storm clouds darkened the winter sky, and each day was colder than the last. Then, the snow came to the colt's prairie, too.

Day after day, it fell—covering the land in a white stillness and burying the colt's favorite grasses under the deep drifts.

The horses chewed on bare branches and tore bark from the trees. The colt's mother searched for food, but there was none to be found.

Desperate, the horses left the prairie to search for food.

As the horses wandered through the forest, the snow began to fall more fiercely.

The wind was so strong that the colt could barely move. He followed in the footprints that his mother left in the deep snow.

The wind blew and blew, and the snowstorm became a raging blizzard. Cold and afraid, the colt huddled against his mother. She nuzzled him with her soft face to help keep him warm.

All around them, the drifts grew deeper.

The anxious colt struggled to keep his head above the snow.

It snowed until the drifts were so deep that the horses couldn't move. Soon they were almost completely buried. And, still the snow came swirling down from the sky.

Until, in the dark of the night, the blizzard finally passed and calm returned to the forest. The stars sparkled in the still night sky, and strange puffs of steam rose from the ground, but the horses were nowhere to be seen.

Slowly, the night turned into morning.

Suddenly, a horse burst through the drifts. He shook the snow from his mane and whinnied in the bright morning light. Then came another. The colt, too, eagerly dug his way out of the snow. His eyes searched the sunny forest for the other horses. The colt's mother was right beside him.

Once more, the horses continued their journey. At the edge of the forest they crossed a river.

The water was cold and the current was strong, but the colt swam close to his mother, and together they made it to the other side.

One by one, the horses followed the banks of the river through a great salt marsh, until, at last they arrived at the sea.

The colt had never seen the sea before. He stood with his mother and watched the waves roll across the sand. They had finally found what they were looking for.

The hungry horses began to eat kelp they found washed up along the shore.
When the colt finished eating, he pranced in the waves and chased the
squawking gulls.

After their feast, the horses galloped along the beach. The colt raced behind them.

He had survived his first winter. Soon it would be spring again, bringing new colts to the herd.

A Note from the Editor

The wild horses depicted in this book are based on the Dosanko horses found on the island of Hokkaido in Japan. The ancestors of these horses, called Nambu horses, were brought to Hokkaido by merchants and fisherman more than three hundred years ago. These merchants and fisherman stayed on the island during the warm seasons, but when winter came they returned to the mainland, leaving the horses to face the harsh winters on their own.

Although some horses did not survive this cycle, those that did survive developed into a new breed—one that was shorter, with longer hair and tougher hooves—the Dosanko. Like many breeds of wild horses, the Dosanko horses remain only in small numbers. Today, there are just over a thousand Dosanko horses in Hokkaido and most of them live on wild horse preserves.

The story in this book is based on a recurring event. When faced with blizzard conditions, the Dosanko horses will lie down on the ground, allowing themselves to be covered by the snow. By doing this, they are protected from the ferocious wind and are able to maintain a warmer body temperature. Over time, there have been frequent reports of Dosanko horses surviving harsh winter storms just as the horses in this story survived their wild winter.